P9-AOI-722

I Am a Good Citizen

by Melissa Higgins

Consulting Editor: Gail Saunders-Smith, PhD

Content Consultant: Susan M. Swearer, PhD
Professor of School Psychology and Licensed
Psychologist; Co-Director, Bullying Research Network
University of Nebraska–Lincoln

CAPSTONE PRESS
a capstone imprint

Pebble Books are published by Capstone Press,
1710 Roe Crest Drive, North Mankato, Minnesota 56003
www.capstonepub.com

Library of Congress Cataloging-in-Publication Data
Higgins, Melissa, 1953–
I Am a Good Citizen / by Melissa Higgins.
pages cm.—(Pebble books. I Don't Bully)
Summary: "Simple text and full color photographs describe how to be a good citizen, not a bully"—Provided by publisher.
Includes bibliographical references and index.
Audience: Age 5–8.
Audience: K to grade 3.
ISBN 9781476540719 (library binding)
ISBN 9781476551753 (pbk.)
ISBN 9781476560403 (ebook pdf)
1. Citizenship—Juvenile literature. I. Title.
JF801.H54 2014
323.6—dc23 2013029181

Note to Parents and Teachers

The I Don't Bully set supports national curriculum standards for social studies related to people and cultures. This book describes being a good citizen. The images support early readers in understanding the text. The repetition of words and phrases helps early readers learn new words. This book also introduces early readers to subject-specific vocabulary words, which are defined in the Glossary section. Early readers may need assistance to read some words and to use the Table of Contents, Glossary, Read More, Internet Sites, and Index sections of the book.

Printed in the United States of America in North Mankato, Minnesota.
092013 007764CGS14

Table of Contents

I Follow Laws and Rules

I respect my country
and my community.
I'm a good citizen.
I don't bully!

Laws help keep me safe. Kids who bully don't obey laws.

STOP
BULLYING
it can
really
HURT

I follow my school's rules.
Kids who bully break rules.
They hit, push, and
act mean.

STOP BULLYING
it can really HURT
so show YOUR true stripes!

I Take Part

I make my school better.
If I know someone is
being bullied, I tell
an adult who can help.

A213
Mrs. Lowry

I listen to my teachers. Kids who bully don't listen to others.

I lend a hand to keep things clean. Kids who bully don't care about making a mess.

I Protect the Earth

I use my school's recycling bins. Kids who bully don't care about helping the earth.

I treat animals with respect.
Bullies can be mean
to animals too.

STOP
BULLYING
it can
really
HURT

I Give More Than I Take

Everywhere I go, I try to make it a better place. That's why I'll never bully!

Glossary

bully—to be mean to someone else over and over again

citizen—someone who lives in a country, state, or city

community—a group of people living together

law—a rule that tells people how to behave

obey—to do what you are told

recycling bin—a place to put materials that can be reused over and over, such as glass, cans, and paper

respect—to treat with proper care